MAY THE VOTES BE WITH YOU

For the aliens who crash-landed into my life: Larry, Ashley, and Austin—L.H.

For David, who made one heck of a young Earthling school president—J.W.

Text copyright © 2017 by Lisa Harkrader
Illustrations copyright © 2017 by Jessica Warrick
Galaxy Scout Activities illustrations copyright © 2017 by Kane Press, Inc.
Galaxy Scout Activities illustrations by Nadia DiMattia

Library of Congress Cataloging-in-Publication Data

Names: Harkrader, Lisa, author. | Warrick, Jessica, illustrator.
Title: May the votes be with you / by Lisa Harkrader ; illustrated by Jessica Warrick.
Description: New York : The Kane Press, 2017. | Series: How to be an earthling ; 7 | Summary: "When Piper runs for student council, she needs the help of the alien Spork in order to add razzle-dazzle to her campaign"— Provided by publisher.
Identifiers: LCCN 2016029833 (print) | LCCN 2016043059 (ebook) | ISBN 9781575658490 (pbk) | ISBN 9781575658452 (reinforced library binding) | ISBN 9781575658537 (ebook)
Subjects: | CYAC: Extraterrestrial beings—Fiction. | Elections—Fiction. | Schools—Fiction. | Humorous stories.
Classification: LCC PZ7.H22615 May 2017 (print) | LCC PZ7.H22615 (ebook) | DDC [Fic]—dc23
LC record available at https://lccn.loc.gov/2016029833

1 3 5 7 9 10 8 6 4 2

First published in the United States of America in 2017 by Kane Press, Inc.
Printed in China

Book Design: Edward Miller

How to Be an Earthling is a registered trademark of Kane Press, Inc.

Visit us online at **www.kanepress.com**

 Like us on Facebook
facebook.com/kanepress

 Follow us on Twitter
@KanePress

CONTENTS

***Don't miss a single one
of Spork's adventures!***

MAY THE VOTES
BE WITH YOU

by Lisa Harkrader
illustrated by Jessica Warrick

KANE PRESS
New York

Spork

Trixie Lopez

Mrs. Buckle

Jack Donnelly

Piper Cho

Grace Hanford

Adam Novak

Newton Miller

Jo Jo

BEEP. BEEP. BEEP.
Greetings, Galaxy Scouts! I've been cleaning out my flying saucer. Maybe I can get my Tidiness Badge!

I found my Junior Varp Zerpingnut helmet. Just putting it on my head makes me feel a little like Varp himself. Like I could lead our planet. Quit laughing. It could happen.

I also found my Star Blitzer. Remember that time at scout camp when we took the Blitzer for a spin? Okay, the spin turned into a splunk. But hardly anybody noticed the missing star. The Little Dipper looks fine without it.

And the Blasteroid Simulator—how fun was that? Hey! Maybe I'll show it to my Earth friends. They always ask what outer space is like.

What could go wrong?

1

ALL TANGLED UP

"Mrs. Buckle!" Piper wobbled into the third-grade classroom. "It's my best idea yet!"

Piper was wrapped in tin foil, her arms piled high with posters and papers. A model of the solar system teetered on top.

"That's quite a load," said Mrs. Buckle.

Piper peered around the stack. "It's my assignment on planets. I know you said to make a poster. But a poster's just something you look at. I wanted to get everyone *involved*. Here's my idea: Every third grader can make their own solar suit! I drew up plans."

Mrs. Buckle smiled. "I can't wait to see."

Piper couldn't wait for *everyone* to see. Especially Spork.

Spork was new in class. He was a space alien who had crash-landed on their playground. Spork knew more about solar stuff than *anybody*.

He and Trixie were pinning their posters to the bulletin board. Piper wobbled toward them.

Jack stared at her. "What are you wearing?"

"It's my test model of a solar energy suit." Piper held up a leg to show him. "It could change how the world gets energy. It could—uhh—ohhh—AHHHH—"

Foil tangled between her feet. Piper tripped, and her project flew from her arms. Papers scattered. The solar system bounced. Neptune popped off and rolled away.

Jack snorted. "Another disaster."

Piper stuck out her chin. "My ideas are not disasters."

"Like your idea to do gym and computer class at the same time?" Jack said. "The computer lab still smells like stinky socks."

"It was a great idea." Piper untangled the foil. "It saved a lot of time. I—I just need to work out a few bugs."

"Yeah, *stink* bugs." Jack held his nose.

Piper sighed. She wanted to change the world. And she *would*. She just needed the right idea.

As Piper peeled off her energy suit, Mrs. Buckle clapped her hands.

"This week is Citizenship Week," she said. "Today we have a special guest to tell us about citizenship. Then we'll take part in some citizenship of our own—student council elections."

"Student council?" said Spork. "That sounds important."

"It is," said Grace.

Piper nodded. Student council was *really* important.

"Each class picks one student to represent them," said Mrs. Buckle. "The candidates will give their speeches on Friday. Then we'll vote."

"We need good candidates," said Newton.

"No problem," Jack said. "I'll run for student council."

Spork's forehead wrinkled. "Do you fit the uniform?"

"What uniform?" asked Jack.

"On my planet, the leader wears a uniform," said Spork. "When we need a new leader, everyone tries it on. The one it fits is the leader. You should see pictures of Varp Zerpingnut. No wonder he was our first leader. His uniform fit perfectly."

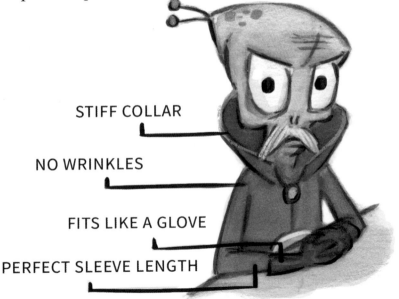

STIFF COLLAR

NO WRINKLES

FITS LIKE A GLOVE

PERFECT SLEEVE LENGTH

"That's nuts." Jack rolled his eyes. "Here's how we do student council. It's a sweet deal. Your friends vote for you. So if you have the most friends, you win. Then you get to skip class to go to the student council meetings. It's like you're the boss of the third grade."

The boss of the third grade? thought Piper. *Jack has it all wrong.*

"You're not the boss," she told him. "And you shouldn't have friends. I mean, you should have friends, but not to vote for you. I mean—"

This wasn't coming out right. She tried again.

"Student council doesn't mean skipping class," she said. "It means *caring* about your class. And your

school. And the whole planet. And—
and other planets. Maybe not all the
planets. You probably won't have time.
But it means speaking up for the third
grade. It means doing your best for
everyone."

Piper took a breath.

Trixie's hand shot into the air. "I
nominate Piper for student council!"

2

A GREAT, UN-STINKY IDEA

Student council? Piper swallowed.

Could she really be on student council?

She slid down in her chair.

Student council was—was—

She stopped. Why hadn't she thought of it before? Student council was a *real* chance to change the world.

"Who knows what *citizenship* means?" Mrs. Buckle was saying.

Piper blinked to attention. She knew this one! "You're a citizen of the place where you live."

"Excellent," said Mrs. Buckle. "But being a good citizen is more than just living in a place. It means taking care of that place."

Spork frowned. "Like feeding it soup when it has the Klozidian flu?"

"Most *places* don't need soup," said Mrs. Buckle. "But people sometimes do. Being a good citizen also means caring about the people around you."

As the third graders talked about citizenship, Mrs. Buckle made a list on the board.

Good Citizens:
Care aboout their community
Care about others
Stay informed
Get involved
Obey laws
Vote

Mrs. Buckle set the chalk down. "We have a very special guest to tell us more about citizenship. Let's welcome our mayor, Eleanor Tupper."

The door opened. A tall woman in cowboy boots and an old-fashioned dress clomped into the classroom.

"Thank you." The mayor swirled her dress. "Today I'm dressed as my great-grandmother, Nell Tupper. Nell was a very good citizen. She helped found our town. She went to town meetings. She listened to her neighbors. She wanted to make the town better for everyone."

Me, too! thought Piper. *Why else would I dress in tin foil?*

"The town needed a school," said Mayor Tupper. "So Nell started one. When the weather was bad, she drove kids to school in her wagon. It was our first school bus."

Mayor Eleanor Tupper

A wagon school bus! That's what Piper needed for student council—a great, un-stinky idea.

"Nell knew voting was important," said Mayor Tupper. "During the town's first election, she drove people to the town hall to vote. When the ballots were counted, the town had elected their first mayor—Nell Tupper."

Spork's eyes grew wide. "Your first leader. Like Varp Zerpingnut."

Piper nodded. *Maybe our first leader is just the inspiration I need to be our* next *leader.*

That afternoon during art class, Trixie and Spork made campaign posters. Piper tried to think up an idea that would get the whole school excited.

As she stared into space, Jack spilled a blob of paint. He grabbed a wad of paper towels to dab it up.

A girl washed her paintbrush. She used *four* paper towels to dry it.

Piper sighed. Using that many was terrible for the planet. Plus, they could buy lots more paint if they didn't spend so much money on paper towels.

Paper towels! Piper blinked.

"That's it!" she said. "Go Green!"

"Green?" Spork stared at his poster. "I made mine red."

"A red poster can say 'Go Green,'" said Piper.

"Red can be green?" Spork lowered his voice. "Does our art teacher know about this?"

Piper laughed. "Going green means trying not to hurt the earth."

"Oh, no." Spork's eyes grew wide. "*I* hurt Earth. I didn't mean to. But when I landed, I crashed into it pretty hard. We need to get some green on me— warp speed."

Trixie patted his arm, then turned to Piper. "Is 'Go Green' exciting enough?"

"It's *super* exciting," said Piper. "We can go paperless. We can do a walking school bus. We can compost food scraps from the lunchroom to fertilize the school garden. We can—"

"Wait!" said Spork. "I'm still drawing the walking school bus. Where do I put the legs?"

"A walking school bus means we walk in a group instead of riding the bus," said Piper. "It saves gas, plus we don't pollute the air."

"A bus that's not a bus?" Spork shook his head. "Being an Earth leader is complicated."

"I still think Go Green should be more exciting. . . ." Trixie snapped her fingers. "What we need is razzle-dazzle."

"Razzle-dazzle?" said Piper.

"Yes!" said Spork. "We should put it on everything. Posters. Flyers. Uniforms. One question: What's razzle-dazzle? Is it like sprinkles? Sprinkles are the best thing Earthlings ever invented. I'm not sure they'd taste good on a poster, though."

"It's kind of like sprinkles," said Trixie. "Only you don't eat it. Razzle-dazzle is something that gets everyone's attention. It makes them say 'WOW!'"

Best
Thing
Ever!

Spork frowned for a moment. Then he zipped to the supply closet. He pulled out paint and clay and wire and a chisel. He lugged them to a corner table and began

working. Clay and paint splattered
everywhere.

Piper looked at Trixie. Trixie
shrugged. "Uh, Spork, what are you
doing?" she asked.

"I'm making"—Spork waved a
paintbrush—"*razzle-dazzle.*"

3

EVERYBODY LOVES HAMSTERS

Piper and Trixie stared at Spork's art project.

It was a giant model of Mount Rushmore—except on one side, next to George Washington, was another face.

"It's . . . *me*." Piper shook her head. It was weird seeing her face up there with all those presidents.

"I don't know why your leaders want
to be squashed into a mountain," said
Spork. "But you should be there, too. I
added a volcano for *extra* razzle-dazzle."

"That is razzle-dazzly," said Trixie.

Piper nodded.

Piper, Trixie, and Spork dragged their
posters—and Mount Rushmore—into
the hall.

Jack's posters already lined the walls.
Each one had a picture of the class
hamster. Jack stood beneath them.

Third graders crowded around him.

"A vote for me is a vote for Jo Jo," Jack told them.

"I love Jo Jo!" said one girl.

"She's so cute!" said another.

"*Jo Jo?*" said Piper.

"Don't worry." Spork patted her shoulder. "I don't think they make uniforms that small."

"If I'm elected," Jack continued, "I'll make Jo Jo our school mascot." He looked up and saw Piper. "See? Piper wants Jo Jo to be our mascot, too. Don't you?"

"No. I mean, yes. I mean—" Piper closed her eyes. This was coming out all wrong. "Jo Jo's great. But student

council isn't about
hamsters."

"You don't like Jo Jo?"
a girl asked.

"That's what she said,"
said someone else.

"That's *not* what I
said." Piper flung her
hand toward a poster.
"I like Jo Jo."

Her flinging hand
bumped Mount
Rushmore. The
volcano gave a
belch, and green
goo spewed
from the top,

showering the hall . . . and the kids.

The third graders shrieked.

"It works!" cried Spork. "It's going green on *everything*!"

"Turn it off!" said Piper.

Spork waved his hand. The volcano burped out one last, enormous blob. It splatted Jack's poster and coated the whole thing—including Jo Jo—green.

The third graders gasped.

"Piper really *doesn't* like Jo Jo," said a boy.

"Yes, I do!" Piper tried to wipe the poster with her sleeve. "This was an accident."

The bell rang. The third graders headed toward class, plucking goo globs from their hair.

"I love Jo Jo," Piper called after them. "I always feed her when somebody forgets."

Nobody listened. Piper was left in the hallway with Spork, Trixie . . . and Mount Rushmore. Piper stared at the presidents' faces. No wonder they all looked so serious. Being a leader was hard.

For the rest of the week, Trixie and

Spork helped Piper give her campaign more razzle-dazzle.

"Nothing that squirts, spurts, or spews," Piper said.

But every time Piper tried to dazzle the class, Jack came up with something bigger, better, and more dazzling.

Piper jazzed up her posters with glitter.

Jack decked his out in blinking lights.

Piper gave everyone sparkly Go Green pencils.

Jack handed out cupcakes with hamster-shaped, glow-in-the dark rings on top.

"And sprinkles," Spork pointed out.

Piper collected lunch scraps. She held compost relays after class.

Jack invited everyone to his house for a pizza party. "We'll have pizza *all* the time if I'm elected," he said.

Grace and Newton stayed for the relays, along with Trixie and Spork. Everyone else went to Jack's.

Piper slumped against the wall.

"Spork's right." She fed a broccoli scrap to Jo Jo. "It would be easier to try on a uniform. Nobody wants to listen to my ideas."

Grace sighed. Newton hung his head. Even Trixie seemed discouraged.

But Spork gave Piper a smile.

"Never fear," he said. "I have a great plan for your speech tomorrow. It's super-sized razzle-dazzle."

4

RAZZLE-DAZZLE

Piper clasped her speech in her hands.

Election day was here. *Finally.* Mrs.
Buckle had set up two chairs on the
cafeteria stage—one for Piper and one for
Jack. Piper sat in hers. She watched the
third graders file into the lunchroom.

Grace and Newton scrambled into seats

in the front row. Trixie and Spork slid in beside them. Spork was clutching a box he'd lugged in from his spaceship that morning. He wouldn't tell anyone what it was.

Piper read through her speech one last time. Trixie had helped her write it. Trixie put in jokes and jazzy slogans. Piper hoped they were dazzly enough to get third graders to listen to her ideas.

Mrs. Buckle strode onto the stage.

"Welcome to the student council speeches," she said. "Our first candidate is a four-foot, eight-inch third grader from Ripley Street. He likes basketball and grilled-banana sandwiches. His favorite subject is recess. Let's welcome *Jaaaaaack Donnelly*!"

Jack swaggered to the microphone. "Thank you. Thank you very much. If I'm elected, I'll make recess longer. I'll make the cafeteria food better. I mean, broccoli? *Blech*. Am I right?"

The third graders laughed.

"And hard desk chairs," said Jack. "Who needs 'em? I'll bring in beanbag

chairs. Beanbags for everyone! Plus, I'll make sure third grade has less reading and more movies."

Grace's mouth dropped open. Piper heard her whisper, "But I *like* reading."

"Me too," Newton whispered back.

"And remember," said Jack, "a vote for me is a vote for—"

"Jo Jo!" shouted the crowd.

Jack swaggered to his seat.

Piper swallowed. It was her turn.

"Our next candidate hails from Juniper Street," said Mrs. Buckle. "She likes French toast and walking her dog. Her favorite subject is . . . all of them! Let's give a warm third-grade welcome to *Piperrrrrrr Cho!*"

Piper made her way across the stage. She saw Spork tugging on the lid of his box.

She took a deep breath. "Thank you." Her voice squeaked. "If you elect me—"

BAM!

Lights flashed. Stadium music blasted through the gym.

BZZZZT!

The solar system blazed to life in 3-D.
It sparkled and whirled in the air.

WHOOOSH!

Meteors streaked across the cafeteria.
Kids shrieked and dove for cover.

Piper blinked. "What—?"

"It's my Blasteroid Simulator," Spork shouted over the noise. He held up a shiny metal ball. "I had razzle-dazzle in my spaceship all along. I just didn't know it."

The class quickly figured out that the meteors were holograms. They climbed from under their chairs and began dodging meteors to the beat of the music. Spork had rolled Mount Rushmore into the lunchroom. Meteors swirled around it.

Spork waved his hand over the metal ball. The meteors flew faster.

He waved again. They changed color.

He waved in a circle. A voice boomed through the gym:

IN A WORLD WHERE A CLASSROOM
NEEDS A LEADER, ONE THIRD GRADER
HAS RISEN TO THE CHALLENGE.
FASTER THAN A SPEEDING METEOR,
MORE POWERFUL THAN JUPITER'S
GRAVITY, PROMISING CUPCAKES AND
SPRINKLES FOR ALL, THAT THIRD
GRADER IS—

"STOP!" Piper shouted. "That's not
why I'm here."

5

AND THE
WINNER IS...

The music stopped. The solar system
faded. The voice rumbled to a halt.

"Well! That was . . . exciting." Mrs.
Buckle helped free a boy who was stuck
under Mount Rushmore. "Let's sit back
down and give Piper our full attention."

The third graders, out of breath,
collapsed into their seats.

"Thanks, Mrs. B." Piper looked out at the class. Everyone seemed happy. They'd loved all that razzle-dazzle.

And suddenly Piper realized that Jack was kind of right. Student council *was* about hamsters. Partly.

Piper had wanted to be a good citizen. She wanted to be like Nell Tupper and make the school a better place. She wanted the third graders to listen to her.

But she had forgotten something. Nell was the one who listened. Nell had listened to her neighbors. She knew what was important to them.

Like hamsters were important to Piper's class.

Piper swallowed. "I can't promise longer recess—"

The third graders grumbled.

"But if we compost our lunch scraps," said Piper, "we can spend more time in the school garden. Maybe we can have science class there sometimes."

The third graders perked up.

"I can't promise a totally delicious lunch," said Piper.

The third graders groaned.

"But," said Piper, "we can have more fresh veggies from our garden. Maybe even broccoli. Because you know who likes it?"

"Jo Jo!" said Trixie.

Spork's eyes grew wide. "A vote for compost is a vote for Jo Jo."

"A vote for Jo Jo *and* for our whole school," said Piper. "We could enter . . . the Go Green Challenge. It's a contest for the most earth-friendly school. First prize is a campout at Wilderness Park."

The third graders clapped.

"With nature walks," said Piper.

The third graders cheered.

"And baby turtles," said Piper. "We'd help release them into the water."

The third graders whooped and hollered.

"That's the best recess *ever*," said Newton.

The third graders went back to their classroom and voted.

Mrs. Buckle wrote JACK and PIPER on the board and tallied the votes under each name.

She frowned. "We have a tie. Eleven votes for Piper. Eleven for Jack."

"We need a tie-breaker," said Grace.

"I have my Junior Varp Zerpingnut helmet," said Spork. "They could try it on and see who fits."

"Thank you, Spork. I think we can solve this without a helmet." Mrs. Buckle turned to the class. "We have twenty-three students, but only twenty-two tallies. Did someone forget to vote?"

The third graders looked at each other.

"Fine," said Jack. "It was me."

Piper stared at him. Jack hadn't voted? That meant . . . she'd *lost*. Jack would vote for himself. He'd win.

Jack turned in his ballot.

Tears prickled Piper's eyes. She blinked them away. She wouldn't cry. She'd shake Jack's hand. And say, "Congratulations." And . . . and help carry out the old chairs when the beanbags arrived. That's what Nell Tupper would do.

Mrs. Buckle unfolded the ballot.

Trixie groaned.

Piper stared at the floor.

Spork leaned over. "I'll still eat broccoli," he whispered.

Piper nodded.

She heard the class gasp.

She looked up. On the board were eleven marks under Jack's name . . .

. . . and twelve under hers.

She turned to Jack. "But—"

"I voted for you, okay?" Jack crossed his arms over his chest. "Running for student council took all my free time. It would take even more if I won. Plus"—his voice got quiet—"I like . . ."

He mumbled something.

"What?" said Piper.

"Turtles, okay?" said Jack. "I like turtles."

"Me too!" said Piper. "Turtles can be

our theme. We'll call our walking school bus the Turtle Express. We'll recycle paper in Turtle Bins. We'll catch rain water for the garden in Turtle Barrels."

Piper stopped to catch her breath.

Spork's eyes grew wide. "That would *really* get some green on me! I'd make up for hurting Earth." He put his arm around Piper Cho, brand-new class leader. "Because, of the twenty-six planets I've crashed into, this one's the best."

GALAXY SCOUTS

BEEP. BEEP. BEEP.

Greetings, Galaxy Scouts!

Guess what I did. I helped my class choose a leader.

Choosing an Earth leader is hard work. You have to draw posters and eat cupcakes and give speeches and carve people into mountains. On top of that, you have to listen to others and think up ideas. Ideas about turtles work best.

At first it seemed a lot different from choosing a leader on our planet. But it turned out kind of the same. We picked the person who best fit the job. I gave her my Varp Zerpingnut helmet.

Now all she needs is a uniform.

ACTIVITIES

Greetings!
*   Wow, Earthlings choose leaders in a different way than we do on my planet! The kids in Mrs. Buckle's class voted for the third grader they think has good ideas, cares the most, and will do the best to represent the class. Cosmic! Take this Citizenship Challenge to see if you'd be a good Galactic Citizen.*
—Spork

(There can be more than one right answer.)

1. Someone sprayed Plasma Paint all over Varp Zerpingnut Park. How can you be a good citizen?
   a. Play at a different park.
   b. Report the damage to the Galactic police.
   c. Try to scrub away the paint to make the park look razzle-dazzly again.
   d. What paint? Ignore it and play there anyway.

2. The Scout Training Center throws away a lot of food after lunch each day. What can you do?
   a. Grab some extra pluppleberries . . . then toss out the rest.
   b. Start a petition to have the extra food donated to hungry Grubzinaks.
   c. Suggest composting the leftovers in the garden.
   d. Bring a lunch from home instead of eating in the cafeteria.

3. Galaxy Scout Council is holding its once-an-orbit election. You:

   a. Read up on each of the scouts in the election.

   b. Offer to help out a friend who is running for the Council.

   c. Run for Council yourself. You want to help improve the galaxy!

   d. Vote for the alien who gave you the super-fancy star blitzer, of course.

4. A big storm damaged your part of the planet. You:

   a. Just stay inside—at least your Blasteroid Simulator still works.

   b. Complain about your power going out. Your house is like a black hole!

   c. Offer to help clean up the town center where many meteors fell during the storm.

   d. Send messages to your friends. They might need help.

Recycling and Composting

Piper has another great Going Green idea! She wants to improve the school by composting leftovers from lunch. Most food scraps, except meat and dairy, can be composted. So can paper goods and cardboard! Other things, like plastic, metal, and glass, can be recycled.

I want to help Piper, but we don't compost or recycle on my planet, so I need your help. Look at the lunch table and make lists of what can be composted and what can be recycled. Oh, and here are some hints about what's in my homemade meal: Pluto potatoes (vegetable), Yorgnak cheese (dairy), and a plastic cup of pluppleberry juice. Yum.

Answers: The juice can, juice bottle, and plastic cup can be recycled. The bread, banana peel, cupcake wrapper, apple core, milk carton, celery sticks, and Pluto potatoes can be composted. The drumstick (meat) and Yorgnak cheese (dairy) should not be composted. (But that's okay—Yorgnak cheese is so yummy, I never have leftovers anyway!) Remember: if you use plastic utensils and paper plates and napkins, they can be recycled, too.

MEET THE AUTHOR AND ILLUSTRATOR

LISA HARKRADER lives and writes in a small town in Kansas. She tries to act like a proper Earthling, but usually feels more like an alien.

JESSICA WARRICK has illustrated lots of picture books about dogs, cats, and kids, but she is mostly interested in drawing aliens, for some strange reason. She does a pretty good job acting like an Earthling . . . most of the time.

Spork just landed on Earth, and look, he already has lots of fans!

★ **Moonbeam Children's Book Awards Gold Medal**
Best Book Series—Chapter Books

★ **Moonbeam Children's Book Awards Silver Medal**
Juvenile Fiction—Early Reader/Chapter Books
for book #1 *Spork Out of Orbit*

"Young readers are going to love this series! Spork is a funny and unexpected main character. Kids will love his antics and sweet disposition. Teachers and parents will appreciate the subtle messages embedded in the stories. The kids in the stories genuinely like each other, which I found refreshing. I will be giving these books to my young friends."—**Ron Roy**, author of A to Z Mysteries, Calendar Mysteries, and Capital Mysteries

"A breezy, humorous lesson in honesty that never stoops to didacticism. The other three volumes publishing simultaneously address similarly weighty lessons—lying, shyness, bullying, and responsibility—all with a multicultural cast of Everykids. . . . A good choice for those new to chapters."
—**Kirkus** for book #1 *Spork Out of Orbit*

"This is a book where readers, kids, and aliens learn together, experiencing how words and choices affect all of us. It's simple, elegant, and very insightful storytelling. *Greetings, Sharkling!* doesn't waste a single page of opportunity."
—**The San Francisco Book Review**

"I'm so glad Spork landed on Earth! His misadventures are playful and sweet, and I love the clever wordplay!"
—**Becca Zerkin**, former children's book reviewer for the *New York Times Book Review* and *School Library Journal*

"Kids will love reading about Spork. Parents, teachers, and librarians will love reading aloud this series to those same kids."—**Rob Reid**, author of *Silly Books to Read Aloud*

How to Be an Earthling
Winner of the Moonbeam Gold Medal
for Best Chapter Book Series!

Respect

Honesty

Responsibility

Courage

Kindness

Perseverance

Citizenship

Self-Control

To learn more about Spork, go to kanepress.com

Check out these other series from Kane Press

Animal Antics A to Z®
(Grades PreK–2 • Ages 3–8)
Winner of two *Learning* Magazine Teachers' Choice Awards
"A great product for any class learning about letters!"
—*Teachers' Choice Award reviewer comment*

Let's Read Together®
(Grades PreK–3 • Ages 4–8)
"Storylines are silly and inventive, and recall Dr. Seuss's *Cat in the Hat*
for the building of rhythm and rhyming words."—*School Library Journal*

Holidays & Heroes
(Grades 1–4 • Ages 6–10)
"Commemorates the influential figures behind important American
celebrations. This volume emphasizes the importance of lofty ambitions
and fortitude in the face of adversity…"—*Booklist* (for *Let's Celebrate Martin
Luther King Jr. Day*)

Math Matters®
(Grades K–3 • Ages 5–8)
Winner of a *Learning* Magazine Teachers' Choice Award
"These cheerfully illustrated titles offer primary-grade
children practice in math as well as reading."—*Booklist*

The Milo & Jazz Mysteries®
(Grades 2–5 • Ages 7–11)
"Gets it just right."—*Booklist,* starred review (for *The Case
of the Stinky Socks*); *Book Links'* Best New Books for the Classroom

Mouse Math®
(Grades PreK & up • Ages 4 & up)
"The Mouse Math series is a great way to integrate math and literacy into
your early childhood curriculum. My students thoroughly enjoyed these
books."—*Teaching Children Mathematics*

Science Solves It!®
(Grades K–3 • Ages 5–8)
"The Science Solves It! series is a wonderful tool for
the elementary teacher who wants to integrate reading
and science."—*National Science Teachers Association*

Social Studies Connects®
(Grades K–3 • Ages 5–8)
"This series is very strongly recommended…."—*Children's Bookwatch*
"Well done!"—*School Library Journal*

KANEPRESS.com